My heart is laughing

WRITTEN BY
Rose Lagercrantz

ILLUSTRATED BY
Eva Eriksson

GECKO PRESS

CONTENTS

....

Chapter 1

This is a story about Dani, who's always happy.
She's unhappy too, now and then, but she doesn't
count those times.

She doesn't like unhappy. It makes her go to
pieces. That's why she makes new endings for
stories with unhappy endings.

Dani's interests are hamsters, doing crafts, sleeping in late, and playing with her friends.

That's when she has friends to play with.

When she started school she didn't know anyone in her class, but she does now.

She knows Meatball and Cushion. And Jonathan who has 146 pets: they're all walking sticks. He thinks they're really cute.

And she knows Vicky as well. Everybody does.

Vicky runs to brush her teeth every five minutes. Her mother is a dentist and gives her fluoride to rinse with every day.

Vicky has been in love with just about all the boys in the class. Poof, just like magic, there she goes again.

Mickey's the same.

This story is about the day they both fell in love with Cushion.

At exactly the same time…

They both decided to ask him if he wanted to go out. They could hardly wait to see which one he'd choose.

"Most likely me," said Mickey, looking very pleased with the big paper heart she had cut out.

"Don't be so sure about that." Vicky started to snip out a heart herself.

Vicky and Mickey always copied each other.

Chapter 2

As soon as it was playtime they ran up to
Cushion and grabbed him.

"I'm your girlfriend, aren't I?" shouted Vicky.

"No, I am!" shouted Mickey.

Cushion shook them off without answering.
He didn't have time. He had to work on his
goal-kicking.

After a little while he came back.

He didn't want to go out with either of them.

He came to ask…

…Dani. He gave her a piece of gum from his pocket.

Then he had to go off and do goal-kicking again.

If his team didn't win every match he got yelled at by his father. Sometimes his father yelled at the coach.

Dani sniffed the gum.

It smelled like raspberries.

When she looked up, Mickey and Vicky had disappeared. They'd run off to play hopscotch.

Dani hurried after them and asked if she could play too, but Vicky didn't answer. She treated Dani as if she was invisible. That's what you say when someone pretends not to see you.

Mickey treated her as if she was a rotten banana.

Dani was sad. More than anything she wanted everyone at school to be nice to her.

"You can have my gum if you like," she said.

"No, thanks," sniffed Mickey. "You're not allowed gum at school."

"Don't you know that?" snapped Vicky as they hurried off to the jungle gym.

Dani stayed where she was and watched them. Then she threw her gum away.

Chapter 3

After playtime Dani couldn't be happy. She
missed her best friend Ella who had moved
to another town. Since then no one had been
allowed to sit at Ella's desk. Not Jonathan, not
Susie, not even…

…Cushion, who came and asked if he could. Dani shook her head.

"Where would Ella sit?" she asked.

Cushion looked surprised.

"I mean when she comes back," said Dani.

"Dani, Dani," sighed the teacher, who had overheard the conversation. "Ella is not coming back."

"You never know," mumbled Dani.

She was not one to give up hope, even when everything seemed hopeless.

Otherwise Dani took things as they came.

On Mondays they had P.E.

On Wednesdays they had spelling.

The best thing about spelling was that you were given a gold star when you got them all right.

And every day at twelve o'clock it was lunchtime.

Chapter 4

In the dining room Dani and Ella had always sat
next to each other. Every day. Right over in the
far corner.

Dani sneaked over there with her lunch. It was
sausages and mashed potatoes.

She wanted to be on her own, to think about
something fun. That was her speciality!

First she thought about all the hamsters she knew.

There was one called Partyboy and another
called Littleboy.

And there were her own hamsters, Snow and
Flake.

Then she thought about all the different places she had been.

Like Rome, where her granny lived.

And the other side of town, where her grandma and grandad lived.

And Northbrook. That's where Ella lived now.

It was the most fun place Dani knew.

It had a park with lots of different kinds of trees. Some are easy to climb and some are a bit harder. When Dani was there visiting they decided to climb the hardest one. It was a tree without a single low branch.

It was so high they had to go and find a chair so they could climb up it. They climbed for hours pretending to be monkeys.

It was around Easter.

A long time ago.

They talked monkey language, which is mostly made of smacking and howling noises.

And they ate bananas, of course, and tried hanging by the tail.

Since they didn't have tails they had to use their
arms and legs.

They left the tree for just a moment to run home and get more bananas.

When they came back the chair was gone.

They had to find another one.

How else would they get up the tree?

They didn't stop playing in the monkey tree until night time. Then they ran home again, singing at the tops of their lungs. Monkey songs, of course.

The moon shone and the trees sighed and a dog barked nearby. And everything was fun, as it always is in Northbrook.

But the next day the other chair had also disappeared. It was a mystery.

Ella's mother scolded them and said they couldn't take any more chairs.

And Ella's extra father agreed with her.

Ella has two fathers. A real one she never talks about and an extra one called Patrick.

Except that Ella calls him Paddy.

Paddy said that chairs belong at home in the kitchen and not in the park.

Dani and Ella stopped playing monkeys and went to play with their hamsters instead.

It was fun, too.

Chapter 5

While Dani sat in the school lunchroom
remembering the fun she'd had in Northbrook,
the teacher came over.

"Why aren't you eating?" she asked.

Dani looked at her plate in surprise. She had forgotten where she was.

"I think you should go and sit with the others."

Dani got up. The teacher picked up her chair. Dani followed reluctantly. Where did the teacher want her to sit?

Oh no! Not between Mickey and Vicky!

"This is not going to go well," Dani mumbled to herself.

She was right.

Mickey and Vicky complained loudly when the teacher put Dani's chair between them.

"Noooooooo," said Vicky. "I'm going to faint."

"But we've decided to sit next to each other till we die!" protested Mickey.

But they didn't make a fuss. They didn't dare.

Dani sat down between them, reached over for the sauce bottle, and squeezed some sauce on her plate.

She had hardly put it down when Vicky took it.

"Look," she said. "I touched the sauce bottle even though Dani's touched it."

As if Dani had a terrible disease!

"Me too," said Mickey and she picked it up as well. "Bleeeeegh!"

Dani pretended nothing was going on.

Chapter 6

Then something even worse happened. Vicky
pinched Dani hard on the arm!

Dani kept pretending that nothing was
happening.

That's what you do when someone does
something stupid, her father had told her.

But soon Mickey pinched her, too. Even harder!

It hurt.

They pinched and pinched till Dani howled and leaped out of her chair.

She took a quick look around, grabbed the sauce bottle, aimed it at Mickey, and squeezed as hard as she could.

Sploosh! it went as the sauce flew out…

…and hit Mickey right in the face.

Dani turned around and aimed at Vicky.

Sploosh! Sploosh!

But this time she missed and the sauce hit the teacher.

Dani gasped…

…and dropped
the bottle.

She ran to the door.

Then she turned to look back.

What had she done?

"Stop," called the teacher. "Stop, Dani!"

But Dani pretended not to hear and rushed
out.

She charged out of the room, left the school,
and ran home.

Chapter 7

The house where Dani lives is on Home Street,
next to the hill.

In winter lots of children play there in the snow.

But now it was spring and the hill was green
with grass and covered in little blue flowers
called scilla.

However, that day Dani wasn't thinking about
flowers.

She didn't even see them. She just wanted to get
inside as fast as she could!

The door to her house was locked. It always
was when her father was at work.
But luckily she remembered that
a key lived under the flowerpot
on the step.

All Dani had to do was pick it up and unlock
the door and go in and kick off her shoes.

One shoe ended up on the hat shelf.

The other one flew off towards the small table
with a vase on it.

The vase fell to the floor and broke.
Dani did too, it felt like. She broke
into pieces.

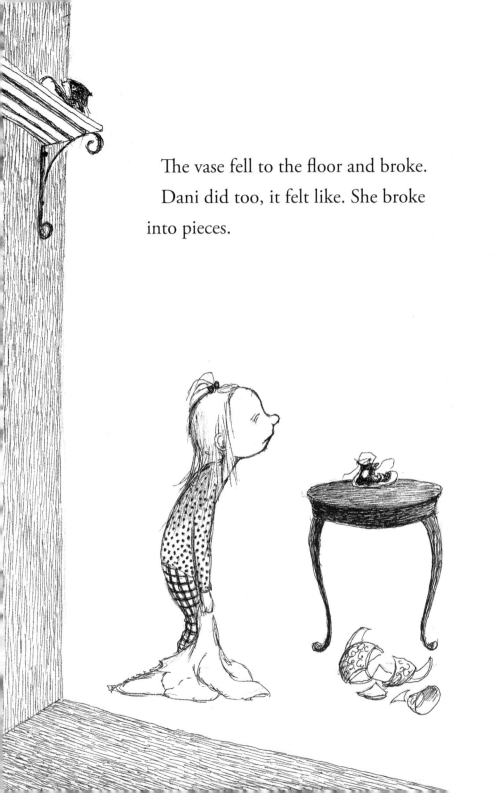

She sank to the floor and started to cry.

First she cried about the vase. Then she cried because she had squirted sauce on the nice teacher. Then she cried because Mickey and Vicky had been so awful.

But most of all she cried because Ella hadn't come back yet.

She cried so hard that her eyes went as red as a white rabbit's.

The hamsters were watching her, worried.
They normally ran around squeaking with
delight, beside themselves with happiness when
Dani came home. But now they sat quite still,
with their paws together, looking at her.

Hamsters are sensitive animals. If they notice that their mother is unhappy, they're unhappy too. And Dani is like a mother to them.

They love her, whatever she does, and they agree with her about everything.

Flake thought it was good that Dani had squirted sauce. You have to defend yourself!

And Snow always likes it when something exciting happens.

But suddenly there was a noise in the hall.

Dani jumped to her feet and put her ear to the door.

Of course, it was her dad!
On Wednesdays he finished early.

Chapter 8

Dani heard the cupboard door open. It squeaked.

Her father was taking out his jogging clothes.

Every Wednesday he went to the park for a run.

There was silence.

And then came footsteps…

Dani quickly turned the bedroom door key.

Just in time!

Her father tried the door handle.

"Dani," he said, "what's the matter? Why aren't you in school?"

Dani kept her lips sealed.

"Are you upset about something?" her father continued.

More silence.

"Is it because of the vase? It's a shame it broke, but that happens. What do you think is more important: my little girl or an old vase? Open the door now, please!"

But Dani wasn't obeying her father any more. That was a new thing about her.

She thought she would never tell him what had happened at school.

She didn't need to because just then the phone rang. Her father left her door and went to answer it.

But soon he was back again.

"Come out now!" he said crossly. "We have to go to school to say sorry to everyone you've squirted sauce on!"

Dani burst into tears and threw herself on the floor.

"I'm dying," she told the hamsters, "and it serves him right!"

The hamsters agreed and ground their teeth, as hamsters do when they're upset.

After a while her father gave up and went away.

Chapter 9

It took a long time before Dani could think about something else. That's what she usually does when she's upset. She thinks about something fun.

Thoughts flew around her head like startled birds, not knowing where to land.

It was a while before she remembered to think about Northbrook. That made her feel a little better.

Northbrook is something you can think about whenever you need to. The only bad thing that happens there is that you have to go home again.

That's how it was for Dani at Easter when she visited Ella.

Right when they were having the most fun, Dani's father came to get her in the car.

They had just finished operating on Ella's dolls and animals and were putting them all to bed when he showed up.

Then it was time to say goodbye and travel back home.

"But shall we have a cup of coffee first?" asked Ella's mother.

"That would be lovely," said Dani's father and he disappeared into the kitchen after her.

Then Ella had an idea.

"Let's run away," she whispered.

So they did. Ella quickly gathered up
everything you need when you are on the
run: a blanket, a hot dog, two pillows, two
toothbrushes, and a few other nice little things
that are good to have.

Dani ran and fetched a book, a packet of
bandages, a pair of scissors, two apples, and two
stuffed animals that were all better now.

They put everything into a sheet and tied it
together to make a big sack.

"We'd better not forget to take a chair with us," said Ella.

Her plan was that they would run to the monkey tree.

They could be sure that no one would find them there.

They sneaked away.

Silently, like thieves in the night.

No one noticed anything.

They were hardly in the tree
before they discovered that they had
forgotten the most important thing:
an umbrella!

Because it started to pour down
rain. They were wet through. The
toys were, too.

In the end they had to run home with their animals so the poor things wouldn't get sick again.

They left behind the wet sheet and tucked all the other things in between two branches.

The rain whipped their faces. It whipped at the grass and the trees and the whole of Northbrook.

And that was the end of running away.

As usual, they forgot the chair.

This time Ella's mother didn't say a word about chairs. She just scolded them for going out in such bad weather.

And Dani's father said they had to say goodbye.

The only thing left to do was to get in the car and put on the seat belt.

Dani would never forget sitting in the back seat staring out at the raindrops on the window. They matched the tears running down her cheeks.

But just as they were about to drive off, Ella came running, wet as a mermaid.

74

"Wait!" she cried. "I forgot your goodbye
present!"

The present was an autograph book, one of those ones where your friends sign their names and write beautiful poems.

But so far all the pages were empty except the first one.

Ella had written on it in her best handwriting:

I am the thorn,
You are the rose.
I've written my name right under your nose.

NEVER forget
your best friend in the world,
Ella

Chapter 10

Every time Dani reads that poem she is happy.
Especially when she gets to the end:

NEVER forget
your best friend in the world,
Ella

   As if Dani
ever would!

Of course sometimes Dani forgets things. For example, her hat and jacket when she leaves school. That happens quite often.

Not to mention her backpack.

She forgets her sports bag, too.

And her homework book. And her packed lunch when they're going on an outing.

Dani certainly is a little forgetful sometimes. Now she had already forgotten why she was cross with her father.

But what was he doing? Why didn't he come and knock on the door again?

Dani got up from the floor, unlocked the door, and put her nose out.

There was a lovely smell!

She followed the smell to the kitchen. There he was, holding a chair out for her.

"*Amore*," he said, "what would you say to two or three or four freshly made pancakes?"

"Yes, please," answered Dani, and she sat down and ate pancakes until she almost burst.

She leant back and closed her eyes. She needed a rest.

But her father had other plans.

"Come on," he said. "They're waiting for us."

"Who are?" asked Dani.

"The teacher and those girls."

Dani couldn't believe her ears. He wasn't going to start all that again!

"Dani," said her father sternly, "you must understand that you can't just squirt sauce at people without saying sorry! We don't do things like that in our family."

He could talk as much as he liked. Dani had no intention of going with him!

But her father wouldn't give up.

"Can you tell me just one thing," he said,
looking her in the eyes. "Why did you do it? You
know what I mean…"

Dani pulled up her sleeves.

Her father went very still.

"What are those?" he asked.

"Pinch marks," she mumbled.

"Pinch marks?" said her dad. "Do you pinch each other in your class?"

Dani shook her head.

"Only Mickey and Vicky…"

She didn't manage to say any more before her father got up and was on his way out to the hall. Without a word he pulled on his jacket and opened the door.

What was he going to do now?

Dani jumped up. It was probably best to go with him after all.

But where on earth had her shoes gone?

She found one on the hat shelf. The other was on the little table where the vase used to be.

"Wait for me!" she shouted and ran after him.

Chapter 11

Dani didn't catch up with her father till they reached the school. He was really angry!

Her dad threw open the door to the classroom and went in. Everything came to a standstill. It was like when you play Statues.

Mickey, who was on her way up to the teacher for help with an equation, came to a sudden stop.

Vicky leaned over her mathematics book.

"I suppose you know why we're here," thundered Dani's father, looking around the room.

No one answered.

In the end Cushion held up his hand. "Because Dani has to say sorry!"

"Wrong!" said Dani's father. "Dani is not going to say sorry. There are some other people here who are going to say sorry!"

He stared at Mickey, but she pretended not to understand.

He looked around for Vicky.

But Vicky was pretending to count.

Then he took Dani, who had hidden behind his back, and pulled up her shirtsleeves.

"Can anyone tell me why Dani looks like this?"

Everyone stared at Dani's arms.

"Look!" he said, pointing. "Look at these bruises! Here and here and here and here…"

The whole class started to move. Everyone wanted to see Dani's bruises, except for Mickey who turned away and headed for her desk.

And Vicky who was turning pages in her book.

The teacher came over to Dani.

She was the person who looked longest at Dani's bruises.

"I see! Now I'm beginning to understand," she muttered.

And you could hear in her voice that she was starting to get as angry as Dani's father.

She shook her head and went over to Vicky and Mickey.

"What does this mean, Michaela?"

"W…we were just playing!" squeaked Mickey.

"Playing!" said the teacher. "Was Dani part of this playing?"

It was quiet for a few seconds.

"No, but Vicky pinched, too…" squeaked Mickey.

The teacher turned to Vicky.

"Is that right, Victoria?"

"I didn't know it would make bruises,"
muttered Vicky.

The teacher stood and looked around the room.

"This is very sad!" she sighed. "Is there anyone else this has happened to?"

It was quiet again.

"Me," said Jonathan finally. "Vicky and Mickey keep pushing me all the time!"

And Susie waved her arm furiously.

"Something sad happened to me!"

She swallowed.

"Yes?" said the teacher.

"My hamster died!"

"But that's not Mickey or Vicky's fault," said Cushion.

"No, but it is sad!"

Then suddenly something unexpected happened.

The classroom door opened again.

And who could it be standing in the doorway but…

Chapter 12

…Ella!

She stood there with
a big smile on her
face!
   A kind of shiver ran
around the desks.
   "What's *she* doing
here?" shouted Benny.
   But Ella didn't
seem to hear. Her
eyes were searching
the room.

When she saw that Dani's chair was empty, her smile disappeared.

"Where's Dani?" she asked.

Dani had lost the power to speak. It was like being in a dream.

In the end she woke up and rushed over to Ella.

Ella let out a happy squeak. "There you are!"

What happened next was that Ella's extra father Paddy poked his head around the door.

"I'm sorry to disturb you," he puffed. "I have an important meeting to go to…"

The teacher gave him a questioning look.

"Here's what happened," he said. "This morning, when I left Northbrook, I thought I was alone in the car. And then I heard someone sneeze!"

"Mmm?" said the teacher.

"It was Ella, hidden under a blanket in the back seat!" said Paddy. "She crept into the car without me noticing. She had to see Dani, she said…"

"Excellent," Dani's father interrupted. "You can leave Ella here. We'll look after her."

The next minute the bell rang. It was time for break.

Everybody hurried out because there are always long lines at snack time. Especially when it's buns or twirls. Or fruit salad or hot dogs or waffles. But that's almost never.

Mostly it's dry biscuits or apples.

They're quite good, too.

Vicky and Mickey tried to sneak out with the others but the teacher stopped them.

"You two stay here!" she said.

Chapter 13

As soon as Dani and Ella reached the dining
room and each had an apple, they rushed to the
table in the farthest corner. Just as they used to in
the old days.

But they weren't left in peace.

Everybody wanted to see Ella and tell her what
had happened since the last time they saw her.

Meatball wanted to tell her how he got hit in the
head by a big block of ice. But Irma said it was
just a small lump of ice.

Susie wanted to talk about her dead hamster.

It was called Hairy.

Jonathan wanted to show her his braces.

Then Cushion and Benny came and wanted everyone to hurry outside, so they could play hide-and-seek.

So that's what they did. It's fun to play when there are lots of people!

Everyone was there except Vicky and Mickey.

They had to stay in the classroom for the whole break and talk to the teacher and Dani's father.

They have a nice schoolyard at Dani's school.

There are two jungle gyms, six slides, two hopscotches, and quite a big field.

But the best thing is the hide-and-seek tree where Cushion stood and counted to a hundred while the others ran and hid.

Dani and Ella rushed to the toolshed, but that
was already taken.

Meatball and Benny were hiding there.

Dani and Ella went on to the blue sand box.
Jonathan was in there.
They ran to the stairs, but there
were lots of children already
under there: Susie, Victor,
Irma, Gabriel, and Jens.

"We can hide behind the tree,"
Ella suggested at last. "Cushion
won't think of looking there!"

But just when Cushion started
looking, the bell rang.
Typical!

Chapter 14

Mickey and Vicky were waiting at the door of the classroom. Now *they* were the ones with red eyes like white rabbits'. You could see how hard they'd been crying. That was because the teacher was going to talk to their parents, but the class didn't know that.

First of all they had to say sorry to Dani. And they didn't want to.

"How long must we wait, I wonder?" said the teacher.

Vicky and Mickey stared straight ahead without answering.

Nothing happened.

Everyone was curious about how the sorry would sound. But some got tired legs from standing and waiting.

"Well?" said the teacher.

What could anyone do? Vicky and Mickey stood as still and quiet as statues.

Until finally Dani said they didn't need to.

"I forgive you anyway," she said.

Everybody breathed out. The drama was over. The class went back into the classroom.

And then Dani's father could finally go off for his run.

Ella sat down in her old place. How lucky it was still empty!

"Dani," she asked, "why do Vicky and Mickey have to say sorry to you?"

"Because I was forced to squirt sauce on them," said Dani.

"Ah, I see," said Ella.

But she didn't at all.

And it didn't matter. The main thing was that no one else had taken her old place.

"This lesson we are going to paint fish," explained the teacher, when the class was quiet. They were having fish and shellfish week.

Dani and Ella each painted a pike with sharp, pointy teeth.

Then the teacher wanted the class
to take out their story books.

MY HAPPY LIFE
was the name of
Dani's book.

It was ages since she'd written
in it. And there didn't seem to be
anything to write about now either.

Dani just sat and waved her pen around and
smiled at Ella, who had been given a sheet of
paper to write on.

"Off you go," said the teacher.

"What shall I write?" asked Dani.

"Write about a time when you were happy," suggested the teacher.

"I'm always happy," said Dani.

That's how it is. She doesn't count the times she's unhappy.

"Write about one of the times when you were *especially* happy then!" said the teacher.

Dani bent over her book.

I am always <u>especially</u> happy when I am with Ella..., she began.

Ella leaned over and read what she had written.

Then she wrote almost the same thing:

I am always <u>especially</u> happy when I am with Dani...

She wasn't copying. Ella never does that.

But she often does the same thing.

Everything was almost the same as it was when they used to sit next to each other every day.

Back then Dani hadn't thought much about how happy she was. She didn't have time to.

She didn't now, either. But she did manage to think: There are probably not many people in the world who like each other as much as Ella and I do!

Then she had to think about what they would do after school.

She hadn't been this happy for a long time!

Dani bent over her story book again and carried on writing.

Then she sat back and looked at the words she had written:

My heart is laughing.

This edition first published in 2014 by Gecko Press
PO Box 9335, Marion Square, Wellington 6141, New Zealand
info@geckopress.com

English language edition © Gecko Press Ltd 2014

First American edition published in 2014 by Gecko Press USA, an imprint of Gecko Press Ltd.
A catalog record for this book is available from the US Library of Congress.

Distributed in the United States and Canada by
Lerner Publishing Group, www.lernerbooks.com

Distributed in the United Kingdom by
Bounce Sales and Marketing, www.bouncemarketing.co.uk

Distributed in Australia by
Scholastic Australia, www.scholastic.com.au

Distributed in New Zealand by
Random House NZ, www.randomhouse.co.nz
A catalogue record for this book is available from the National Library of New Zealand.

First published by Bonnier Carlsen, Stockholm, Sweden
Published in the English language by arrangement with Bonnier Group Agency, Stockholm, Sweden
Original title: *Mitt hjärta hoppar och skrattar*

Text © Rose Lagercrantz 2012
Illustrations © Eva Eriksson 2012

The cost of this translation was defrayed by a subsidy from the Swedish Arts Council,
gratefully acknowledged.

Translated by Julia Marshall
Edited by Penelope Todd
Typesetting by Vida & Luke Kelly, New Zealand

Printed in China by Everbest Printing Co Ltd, an accredited ISO 14001 & FSC certified printer

Hardback (USA) ISBN: 978-1-877579-52-3
Paperback ISBN: 978-1-877579-51-6
E-book (MOBI) ISBN: 978-1-927271-22-3
E-book (EPUB) ISBN: 978-1-927271-21-6

For more curiously good books, visit www.geckopress.com